William Is My Brother

William Is My Brother

by Jane T. Schnitter

illustrated by Gerald Kruck

Perspectives Press
P.O. Box 90318
Indianapolis, IN 46290-0318

Perspectives Press
P.O. Box 90318
Indianapolis, IN 46290-0318

Manufactured in the United States of America

ISBN 0-944934-03-X

Library of Congress Cataloging-in-Publication Data

Schnitter, Jane T., 1958-
    William is my brother / by Jane T. Schnitter ; illustrated by
Gerald Kruck.
        p.   cm.
    Summary: Two young brothers are the same in many ways except that
one was born into the family and the other was adopted.
    ISBN 0-944934-03-X : $10.95
    [1. Brothers—Fiction. 2. Adoption—Fiction.] I. Kruck, Gerald,
ill. II. Title.
PZ7.S36435Wi 1991
[E]—dc20   90-21364
                                                   CIP
                                                   AC

To my husband, Paul, and to my children,
P J, Corey, Emily and Megan

My name is Tony. William is my brother. We both have the same parents, but I was born to them and William was adopted.

I grew inside of our mother, and, when it was time, she gave birth to me. William grew inside of another woman, and she gave birth to him. So when William was born, he had a different set of parents. They are called his birth parents.

When William could understand that he didn't grow inside of our mother, he was sad. He cried.

He said to our mother, "I wish I could have grown inside of you like Tony did."

She said, "That would have been nice. I would have liked that. But that is not the way it happened. My love for you grew inside of me, though, and that is the important thing."

Then William was happy again.

William has a favorite story. It is about when he was adopted. "Tell me about when you got me," William always says. Then William snuggles up close to Mom and she tells him the story.

When William was born, his birth parents knew they couldn't give him the family life they wanted him to have. So they asked an adoption agency to help them find him a home. This is what an adoption agency does.

One day, Mom and Dad got a phone call telling them they had a son. It was William. We drove out to pick him up.

We were very excited and very happy. We took William home and he became part of our family. So William is my brother.

Sometimes William and I play together. And sometimes we fight. That is just because we are brothers.

William and I are different. He has brown hair and I have black hair. He has freckles and curly hair. I have no freckles and straight hair. William can play the piano and I can paint wonderful pictures.

William and I are the same. We both have dark brown eyes. We both love to play video games and hate broccoli. We both like to play ball, ride bikes and read books.

So William and I are different in some ways and the same in other ways. Just like all brothers.

Our dad has curly hair like William's. Sometimes, people look at William's curly hair and then they look at Dad's curly hair. They say, "I know who William gets his curly hair from."

He didn't get his curly hair from our dad. He got it from his birth parents. Sometimes we tell them and sometimes we don't. But we always laugh.

Some people tell William that he is lucky to have us. We think we are lucky to have William.

Some people tell William that he is special because he was adopted. William is not special because he was adopted. William is special because he is William. Just like I am special because I am Tony. And you are special because you are you.

William and I have a secret. It is a great big, wonderful secret. But Mom says it won't be a secret for long.

Soon we will be getting a new sister. Our family will adopt her, too.

We can hardly wait!

Let Us Introduce Ourselves...

Perspectives Press is a narrowly focused publishing company. The materials we produce or distribute all speak to infertility or child welfare issues. Our purpose is to promote understanding of these issues and to educate and sensitize those personally experiencing these life situations, professionals who work in infertility, adoption and fostercare, and the public at large. Perspectives Press titles are never duplicative. We seek out and publish materials that are currently unavailable through traditional sources. Our titles include...

Perspectives on a Grafted Tree

An Adoptor's Advocate

Understanding: A Guide to Impaired Fertility for Family and Friends

Our Baby: A Birth and Adoption Story

The Mulberry Bird: Story of an Adoption

Real For Sure Sister

Filling in the Blanks: A Guided Look at Growing Up Adopted

Sweet Grapes: How to Stop Being Infertile and Start Living Again

Where the Sun Kisses the Sea

Residential Treatment: A Tapestry of Many Therapies

Our authors have special credentials: they are people whose personal and professional lives provide an interwoven pattern for what they write. If **you** are writing about these issues, we invite you to contact us with a query letter and stamped, self addressed envelope so that we can send you our writers guidelines and help you determine whether your materials might fit into our publishing plans.

Perspectives Press
P.O. Box 90318
Indianapolis, IN 46290-0318

About The Author. Jane Schnitter was born and raised in Buffalo, New York, marrried her high school sweetheart, and then moved to Ohio, where she attended Ohio State University. Her husband's job soon had them moving again, this time to Reading, Pennsylvania, where they were foster parents to a total of eight children over a three year span. The Schnitters have four children of their own, two boys who were adopted and two girls who were born to them. This book was written for the Schnitter children, to help them understand the adoptions.

About The Illustrator. Gerald Kruck has always nurtured a passion for illustrating children's books. He has written and illustrated stories for children's magazines and educational books, working as well as an advertising artist. Gerald and his wife have three children and three grandsons, all of whom share his love for children's literature.